Spaghetti Eddie

By
Ryan SanAngelo

Illustrated by
Jackie Urbanovic

Boyds Mills Press
Honesdale, Pennsylvania

Boyds Mills Press, Inc.
815 Church Street
Honesdale, Pennsylvania 18431
Printed in China

Library of Congress Cataloging-in-Publication Data

SanAngelo, Ryan.
Spaghetti Eddie / by Ryan SanAngelo ;
illustrated by Jackie Urbanovic. — 1st ed.
[32] p. : col. ill. ; cm.
Summary: Eddie's love of spaghetti turns him into a hero when he not
only solves neighbors' problems through ingenious use of noodles, but
stops a robber cold with a well-thrown meatball.
ISBN 978-1-56397-974-3 (hc)
ISBN 978-1-59078-778-6 (pb)
1. Spaghetti—Fiction. I. Urbanovic, Jackie. II. Title.
[E] 21 2002 AC CIP
2001091724

First edition
First Boyds Mills Press paperback edition, 2009
The text of this book is set in 16-point Souvenir Medium.

10 9 8 7 6 5 4 (hc)
10 9 8 7 6 5 4 3 2 1 (pb)

To Mom, Dad, Dave, and Chad,
the best family a guy could have,
oh, yeah,
and to rock n' roll!
—R.S.

For my family,
who always thought of me as an artist, and made this possible . . .
And for the continuing support of my dear friends,
who keep me going.
—J.U.

This is Eddie.
He eats spaghetti every day except Sundays.
On Sundays, he eats ravioli.

One afternoon, Eddie's mother sent him to the grocery store to buy frosting for a birthday cake. It was Eddie's father's birthday. The family was throwing a surprise party for him.

Outside, Eddie saw his neighbor Ms. Grier,
sitting on the curb. She was frowning at her shoes.
"What's the matter?" Eddie asked.
"My shoelace broke," Ms. Grier said sadly.
"Now my shoe won't stay on, so I
can't finish my daily run!"

Eddie wanted to help.
He grabbed a spaghetti noodle from his bowl.
"Here," he said to Ms. Grier.
"Use my spaghetti for a shoelace."

"That sounds awfully silly," said Ms. Grier.
But she took the spaghetti noodle anyway.

At the fishing pier, Eddie saw
his friend Mr. Jonathan. "Eddie, my boy!"
cried Mr. Jonathan. "I promised Mrs. Jonathan
I'd catch some fish for dinner,
but my fishing rod broke!"

Eddie wanted to help.
"I'll use my spaghetti noodles
to make a fishing net!"
Eddie told Mr. Jonathan.

"This seems awfully silly," said Mr. Jonathan.
But he took the spaghetti fishing net anyway.

A little later, Eddie heard someone call his name.
It was Adam, an older boy who lived
across the street from him.
"Eddie! I need help!" cried Adam.
"I was jamming with the band
and I broke my guitar strings.
I can't play my guitar without strings!"

Eddie wanted to help.
He counted *one, two, three, four, five, six*
extra-long noodles and pulled them from his bowl.
"Here," he told Adam.
"String your guitar with my spaghetti."

"This seems awfully silly," said Adam.
But he took the spaghetti strings anyway.

Near the grocery store,
Eddie heard people shouting.
A robber ran out of the store,
clutching a big bag of money.

Eddie wanted to help.
He reached into his bowl.
All of his noodles were gone.

Eddie grabbed the meatball from his bowl.
He threw it as hard as he could.

Splat! Eddie's meatball hit the robber
right between the eyes.
"I can't see!" the man screamed.
He ran smack into a tree.

A few minutes later, a policeman came.
Eddie's neighbors told the policeman what had happened.
"Nice throw, kid," said the policeman.
Then he hauled the robber away.

Eddie bought a can of chocolate frosting
in the grocery store. It was almost five o'clock!
He knew his mother would be upset if he was late
for the party, so he ran home as fast as he could.

Nobody was more surprised
by the surprise party than Eddie.

Ms. Grier was there,
telling Eddie's sister about the amazing
spaghetti shoelace.

Mr. and Mrs. Jonathan were there,
telling Eddie's mother about the incredible
spaghetti fishing net.
They had a potful of freshly boiled fish.

Adam was there with his band,
playing "Happy Birthday" Italian-style.

Half the neighborhood was there,
telling Eddie's father how Eddie had stopped a robber
with a single meatball.

Everybody sang "Happy Birthday."
Everybody ate freshly boiled fish.
Everybody had birthday cake with chocolate frosting.
And everybody ate Eddie's father's favorite food.

Spaghetti!